THE CIRCLE

Written by

T.C.H. The Author

Character breakdown

Ashley: The careless wild girl. She does what she wants, when she wants, and to whomever she wants. A bold, overly confident, fearless know it all; yearning for the love she's never had.

Laylah: The caring, independent, no nonsense taking, best friend to Ashley. She has high hopes for herself and her friends; and always tries to see the best in others. She is a positive role model to those around her; but when provoked, she can be a true firecracker.

Tianna: The fake friend who is motivated by greed and money and always leeching off other people. She lacks empathy towards others and if it doesn't benefit her, then she isn't interested.

Amanda: The smart mouth girl who thrives off instigating and creating negative energy.

Jasmine: The intelligent, confident, funny, animated character who lives in her own world and follows her own rules. She's determined to be successful; and refuses to settle for anything less.

Shakayla: The rude, bossy girl who loves drama and seeks validation from others to boost her own ego; down to fight anyone at any time, over anything.

The Circle

T.C.H. The Author

copyright © 2019 by T.C.H The Author
All rights reserved.
Published ℗ in the United States by
T.C.H. The Author

ISBN 978-0-9985032-2-6

eBook ISBN 978-0-9985032-3-3

STORY BREAKDOWN

Welcome to Q-Town, where you will meet Ashley and her circle of "friends." A Group of girls that will ultimately discover that bonds can be tested when betrayal starts to surface, and people's true colors are shown. When negativity begins to rise and egos begin to crash; long term friendships begin to tarnish, and words and rumors that are fueled by hate and envy begin to take on a new life of their own; causing real life to be altered in the worst way. As the story progresses, you will learn to appreciate the value of true friends while keeping a watchful eye out for the fake ones. Welcome to "The Circle."

<u>ASHLEY</u>

<u>The careless wild girl. She does what she wants, when she wants, and to whomever she wants. A bold, overly confident, fearless know it all; yearning for the love she's never had.</u>

<u>Laylah</u>

<u>The caring, independent, no nonsense taking, best friend to Ashley. She has high hopes for herself and her friends; and always tries to see the best in others. She is a positive role model to those around her; but when provoked, she can be a true firecracker.</u>

<u>TIANNA</u>

T

<u>he fake friend who is motivated by greed and money and always leeching off other people. She lacks empathy towards others and if it doesn't benefit her, then she isn't interested.</u>

AMANDA

The smart mouth girl who thrives off instigating and creating negative energy.

WELCOME INTO THE CIRCLE

<u>Dedicated to the circle of friends and the circle of possibilities that makes the circle of life more meaningfully important. Through true friendship; the circle will always remain.</u>

SHAKAYLA

The rude, bossy girl who loves drama and seeks validation from others to boost her own ego; down to fight anyone at any time, over anything.

JASMINE

The intelligent, confident, funny, animated character who lives in her own world and follows her own rules. She's determined to be successful; and refuses to settle for anything less

THE CIRCLE

Written by

T.C.H. The Author

Scene 1: Ashley and Laylah are talking while Laylah does Ashley's hair

Ashley - I like girls that like girls.

Laylah - Girl! What about Jordan? I Thought you were still dealing with him.

Ashley - Let's just say things didn't work out.

Laylah - Wack sex huh?

Ashley - Girllll!! You have NO idea! Not only couldn't he get it up or satisfy me, but he also had boring conversation.

Laylah - (Shaking her head) Damn! All that fineness gone to waste.

Ashley - Bitch that's why I need me a sexy woman. Maybe two...

Laylah - Oh, (Raises eyebrow) now look at you, fantasizing about indulging on the other side.

Ashley - Yeah, I've been thinking about it for a while now.

Laylah - Yassss Girl!! Join the dark side! (Starts laughing)

Ashley - (Starts laughing) I hate you bitch!!

Laylah - You need to hate your stylist enough to never let her touch this head of yours again! (Bursts out laughing more)

Ashley - Oh no bitch; you ain't shit!

Laylah - No, she ain't shit for doing this to you. She needs her license revoked, immediately!

Ashley - (Looks back) You know what Lay? I can't with you.

Laylah - (Turns Ashley's head back to face forward) Be still girl, I'm almost done.

Ashley - So tell me, what's it like being with another girl?

Laylah - Girlllllll!! It is SO exciting! Intense with passion, and never a dull moment...and the sex is incredible!! I'm getting turned on just thinking about it!! (Takes a deep breath and shutters)

Ashley - Oh my god Lay. You're so nasty! (Tries to look disgusted but is actually blushing)

Laylah - (Gets finished with Ashely's hair) Ok girl, you're finally done. Do me a favor and NEVER go back to that non styling stylist again; because if you do, I'll kill you myself. I promise!

Ashley - (Gets up and looks in the mirror) Oh my god Lay!! You slayed my hair! You're my official stylist now!!

Laylah - (Smiles with joy) Glad you like it babes. You're about to make a killing at the club tonight.

Ashley - You know what Lay? I don't even feel like going out tonight. Let's just stay in and watch Movieflix.

Laylah - Ouuuuhhhhh movie night!!! I'll get the popcorn ready for us. Hold on, I'll be right back. (leaves the room and goes downstairs)

<u>Scene 2: Tianna stops by to visit</u>

<u>Tianna</u> - (Knocks on the door)

<u>Laylah</u> - (Ignores the door, fixes popcorn while humming a song from the late '90s)

<u>Tianna</u> - (Knocks on the door and gets fed up, pulls out her phone and video calls Laylah)

<u>Ashley</u> - (Sees Laylah's phone light up, and answers the call) What do you want ugly?

<u>Tianna</u> - Ummmm not you bitch! You look cute though, where are you about to go?

<u>Ashley</u> - Nowhere, just sitting here waiting for Lay to come back up with our popcorn...what you doing girl? Where you at?

<u>Tianna</u> - Bitch! I'm outside of Lay's house. Tell her I'm outside and to come open the door.

<u>Ashley</u> - (Hangs up the call, and dramatically screams downstairs) Layyyyyyyyyyyyyyyyyyyyyyyyyyyy!!!

<u>Tianna</u> - I know this bitch did not hang up on me!

<u>Laylah</u> - (Screams upstairs) Girl! Wwwhhhhhaaaatttttttttt??

<u>Ashley</u> - (Screams back downstairs) Tiannaaaaaaaaaaaaaaaaaaaaaaaaaa's outsideeeeeeeeeeeeeeeeeee!!

<u>Laylah</u> - (Puts the popcorn bag in the microwave, and walks to her front door) Go away, nobody here likes you.

Tianna - Girl if you don't open this damn door!

Laylah - (Starts laughing) Nah, I gotchu boo. Hold on. (opens the door and walks back to the kitchen)

Ashley - (Screams back downstairs) Tiannaaaaaaaaaaaaaaaaaaaaaaaaaa's outsideeeeeeeeeeeeeeeeee Lllllaaaayyyyyy!!

Laylah - (Screams upstairs) I knowwwwwwwwwwwwwww; shesssss's hereeeeeeee nowwwwww!!

Tianna - (Screams upstairs) hiiiiiiiiiiiii bitchhhhhhhhhhhhhhhhhhhhh!!

Ashley - (Screams downstairs) Goooooooooooo awayyyyyyyyyyyyyyyyyyyyyyyyyyy!

Laylah - Y'all stupid for real. Can you say issues?

Tianna - Uhhh bitch! I really need to talk to you. It's really important!

Laylah - (thinking to herself) "I bet this bitch is about to ask me for some money."

Scene 3: Tianna asks Laylah for money

Laylah - It better be important enough to justify why you're here interrupting my movie night. (Gives Tianna the side eye while opening the refrigerator) Don't tell me you and that boy broke up again.

Tianna - Nooooo, and "that boy's" name is Robert. Thank you very much! (Rolls eyes)

Ashley - (Walks downstairs and heads into the kitchen) Lay, girl what's taking so long?

Tianna - (Rolls eyes) Ewww Ashley, go back upstairs! Nobody asked you to come down here.

Ashley - (Gasps) Or! How about you take your ugly ass home. (Shrugs)

Tianna - (Looks around) Bitch, ugly where? Everything about me is on fleek. Why you hating?

Ashley - I guess it's a hard pill to swallow knowing that the mirror keeps lying to you.

Tianna - Bitch, go somewhere. You don't need to be in grown folk's business anyway.

Laylah - (Laughing)

(Microwave stops)

Ashley - (Walks to the microwave, gets out the popcorn, and pours it into a bowl) Lay hurry up; we still gotta find a movie to watch. (Walks past Tianna without saying another word)

Laylah - Bitch you ain't cute! Tryna look all sexy. For what?! (Smiles at Ashley)

Tianna - Right. Walking around like a boxing showgirl.

Ashley - Girl Bye, you wish you looked this good! (strikes a pose and walks upstairs)

Laylah - Her little conceited ass. (Sits down at the kitchen table) Ok girl. Tell me what's going on.

Tianna - I got into a little situation.

Laylah - What you mean... situation? What kind of situation this time Tianna?

Tianna - A situation.

Laylah - Girllll, you pregnant?! Oh my god, Tianna when?!

Tianna - No Girl!! Don't you wish that negative shit on my life!

Laylah - (Giggles) Nah, ok. So, what is it then bitch? You need some money huh?

Tianna - Yes.

Laylah - (Laughing) And, you expect me to give it to you? No bitch. You're always blowing it on dumb shit. I love you but I can't. Besides, Ashley asked me to pay for her license.

Tianna - Ugh! You're always doing something for Ashely! Ashley this, and Ashley that. It's always about fucking Ashley!

Laylah - Bitch! Now you know that Ashley is bae. (Starts blushing) She just doesn't know it yet.

Tianna - Ewww (Rolls eyes) your lesbian ass is so nasty.

Laylah - Yup and proud of it. (Starts licking her lips) There's nothing like the taste of fresh pussy on my face. (Closes her eyes and exotically moans)

Tianna - Ewww. Too much information! So, are you going to give me the money or what?

Laylah - Damn girl! Why are you always begging? Do I look like your mother?

Tianna - Yup.... So mother, can I get some money, please?

Laylah - Ugh! Girl you agi! Bitch you owe me! (Goes into her pocket and pulls out a 100-dollar bill and gives it to Tianna) I want my money back!

Tianna - You love my agi ass though.

Laylah - Unfortunately.

Tianna - So, what are we doing about Tasha's party?

Laylah - Girl, I don't know. You know Ashley doesn't really deal with Tasha after they fought.

Tianna - Girl, Who Cares? She's just going to the party. She doesn't have to be the bitch's best friend.

Laylah - True. You're right. I mean it would be nice for her to just show up at least. After all, it is going to be her birthday party. But then again...you know Ashley is like a short-fused firecracker.

Tianna - Girl, she be the main one starting shit, with all that mouth she got.

Laylah - Leave Bae Alone. I'll talk to her to see what she says. Matter of fact, I'll bring it up tonight when we watch the movie that you're currently so rudely interrupting.

Tianna - Just say you want me to leave, and I'll leave bitch!

Laylah - Ok……leave. Now!

Tianna - Girl bye. (Gets up from the table) I'ma let you finish your little nightcap with Ashley. I know you're trying to shoot your shot. (Starts laughing)

Laylah - Girl you don't know anything. (Gets up from the table smiling)

(Laylah walks Tianna to the door)

Tianna - I appreciate you giving me this money and helping me out with my situation.

<u>Laylah</u> - Girl you know you my bitch! I'll do anything for you. You just better pay me back next week when you get paid from Taco Island.

<u>Tianna</u> - Un uh bitch; you mean Taco Bell!

<u>Laylah</u> - Yeah, Taco Fantasy. That's what I said. (Starts laughing)

<u>Tianna</u> - Ok. I see you got jokes.

<u>Laylah</u> - No, I speak truth. You got jokes. Working at The Crunchy Taco.

<u>Tianna</u> - Bitch bye. (Walks out the door) I'm going to call you later.

<u>Laylah</u> - Alright girl. (Closes the door and walks back into the kitchen)

<u>Scene 4: Laylah talks to Ashley about going to Tasha's party</u>

<u>Ashley</u> - (Screams downstairs) Layyyyyyyyyyyyyyyy; huryyyyyyyyyyy upppppppppppppp!

<u>Laylah</u> - I know this bitch is not rushing me. (Puts another bag of popcorn in the microwave)

<u>Ashley</u> - (Surfs through Movieflix looking for a movie)

<u>Laylah</u> - (Waits for the popcorn to get finished and randomly starts twerking)

Ashley - (Lays back on the bed looking up at the ceiling) I wish this girl would hurry up.

Laylah - (Thinks of how to tell Ashley she likes her)

Ashley - (Gets bored, and starts going through Laylah's phone, looking at her pictures) Aww. I remember this one.

Laylah - (Takes the popcorn bag out the microwave and heads upstairs)

Ashley - (Still looking through Laylah's pictures)

Laylah - (Tiptoes into her bedroom and watches Ashley going through her phone and begins to smile)

Ashley - (Still scrolling through Laylah's pictures) Awww; she still has this one from when we were in the 1st grade. Aww that's my bitch! I swear I love her!

Laylah - (Smiles hard) Love you too babes.

Ashley - (Gets startled and drops the phone on her face)

Laylah - (Laughs as she walks to the bed and hands Ashley the bag of popcorn)

Ashley - How long have you been standing there?

Laylah - Long enough to hear everything you were saying.

Ashley - I can't believe you kept those pictures. They were so long ago.

Laylah - Girllllll; in life all we have are memories. So, it's important to always be able to look back and reflect on how far we've come. That's why I kept them. I look at them from time to time, and it always brings joy to my heart.

Ashley - Yassss bitch! We've been friends for a long, long, long time. Do you remember the pact we made in 3rd grade? We agreed that we weren't going to have boyfriends until we got married.

Laylah - Yeah, I remember. (Laughs) Some pact that was right?

Ashley - Lay, promise me something.

Laylah - Anything babes; what's up?

Ashley - No matter what happens between us; promise me that we'll always be friends.

Laylah - Of course, Ashley, we're friends forever, first, and foremost; no matter what happens or what transpires between or around us. We're friends forever.

Ashley - (Takes the popcorn and pours it into the bowl)

Laylah - Bitch! (Pauses for a second) Your greedy ass ate a whole bag of popcorn by yourself?

Ashley - You were taking so long talking to that leech Tianna and I got hungry. Besides, I figured you were going to bring more because you're just considerate like that...and violà; you did just that. (Starts laughing)

Laylah - (Picks up the pillow and smacks Ashley with it)

Ashley - (Drops popcorn and looks shocked that she got hit with a pillow) Bitch……

Laylah - (Laughs) That's what you get; popcorn breath.

Ashley - Shut up!

Laylah - So, what movie are we gonna watch? (Thinks of how to tell Ashely about Tasha's party)

<u>Ashley</u> - You know your picky ass won't watch the movies I like to watch, and I didn't wanna hear your big mouth bitching at me about the movie I picked...(Rolls eyes) so I didn't pick anything. I was looking though.

<u>Laylah</u> - Awwww, how sweet, you thought about my feelings for once! Awwwww Bookie!!

<u>Ashley</u> - No bitch. I just didn't want to hear your mouth. You talk too much……. Just playing, just playing.

<u>Laylah</u> - You better be playing; so let's pick a movie to watch.

<u>Ashley</u> - K. (Leans back and lays on Laylah)

<u>Laylah</u> - (Puts arms over Ashley)

<u>Ashley</u> - (Smiles and scrolls through movies to watch)

<u>Laylah</u> - Sooooooo....ummmmm...I have to ask you a question, but I don't know what your response will be.

<u>Ashley</u> - Let's find a movie first.

<u>Laylah</u> - Ok. (Hugs Ashley tighter)

<u>Ashley</u> - (Starts blushing more while continuing to look for a movie) Uugghh!! There is nothing on here to watch!

<u>Laylah</u> - I'm sure there's a movie about girls to watch.

(Both become silent for a few seconds)

Ashley - Yeah about that...I'm sure nobody would want to watch that.

Laylah - Girlllllllllll! You are so wrong. We don't even have to watch movies. There are a million different shows we can watch.

Ashley - There aren't too many shows worth watching besides Girlfriends, Living Single, and ummmm, The Circle.

Laylah - Yeah. The Circle sounds like a good show. Let's look it up.

Ashley - (Tries to find The Circle) It's not even on here yet.

Laylah - It will be soon. But in the meantime, let's watch Empire; No! Let's watch Power. No, ummm... let's watch a scary movie and I'll hold you if you get scared. (Looks down at Ashley and winks)

Ashley - Alright, you better. (Picks a Horror movie to watch)

(They Start watching the movie)

Laylah - (Thinks of how to ask Ashley about the party) Babes; Latasha is throwing a party for her birthday, and she wants us to be there.

Ashley - (Ignores what Laylah said and continues watching the movie) Girl this a good movie so far.

Laylah - Bitch! I know your ass heard me!

Ashley - I want some more popcorn. (Gets up, puts the movie on pause, and walks downstairs without acknowledging the question)

Scene 5: Laylah calls Tianna to tell her it's a no on the party

Laylah - Ughhhhh! This girl is gonna make me kill her! (Gets up and walks downstairs after Ashley)

Ashley - (Takes food out of the refrigerator to cook)

Laylah - (Walks up in the kitchen) Bitch; what you finna do? Let me get ready to call the fire department!

Ashley - (Looks back at Laylah) Why are you down here?

Laylah - I'm down here because you're down here, and I live here.

Ashley - Go back upstairs; you aren't needed down here.

Laylah - (Rolls eyes) So are you coming with me to Tasha's party or what?

Ashley - Ewww... (Rolls eyes) Who is Tasha?

Laylah - You only know one Tasha bitch. (Rolls eyes)

Ashley - Oh. (Twists lips) You mean the no good friend who steals other people's boyfriends and then lies about it to keep from getting her ass whopped? Oh! (Speaks in Chinese accent) Nope! I don't know her at all. (Shrugs)

Laylah - (Starts laughing) Girl! You are so stupid!

Ashley - No for realz. I'm not going to her party and I'm not kissing nobody's ass. Sorry. Not sorry.

Laylah - You act like you have to be best friends with her. All you have to do is say "hi" and "bye." That's it.

Ashley - First of all; she's gonna say "hi" to my fist, and then she's gonna say "bye" with my Nike print all over her face.

Laylah - Ashley! Be nice!

Ashley - Now you know I can't stand that bitch! Why would you even ask me to go?

Laylah - Because 1.) (Holds up one finger to count) I thought you would go based upon the fact that I'm going, and 2.) (holds up another finger) I thought that knowing you would be with me would be enough; but I guess I was wrong. (Rolls eyes and walks out of the kitchen) And bitch I don't know why you're taking stuff out to cook; you know your ass can't cook to save your life.

Ashley - (Rolls eyes) Whatever HATER!

Laylah - Ughhhhh. (Walks upstairs to her bedroom and sees Tianna video calling; answers the call) What do you want now? Haven't you caused enough trouble for one night?

Tianna - Girl, you love me. So, did you talk to Ms. Attitude about going to Tasha's Party?

Laylah - Yeah, I just got into an argument with her about it.

Tianna - Why? What did she say?

Laylah - What do you think she said? She said "no", and not only did she say "no"; but she also insinuated that she would throw hands with Tasha if and when she saw her.

Tianna - She is so damn petty I swear! I see she still isn't letting what happened go.

Laylah - Yeah, you know that girl hold grudges all the way to the grave. Makes no damn sense.

Tianna - So is she going to come or what? Because I already told Tasha Y'all were coming.

Laylah - Bitch! How are you speaking and making decisions for us?

Tianna - Because, Y'all are my bitches, and we don't let each other go anywhere alone.

Laylah - Yeah ok Tianna. Your ass is gonna be in hell alone if you keep lying on our names. You need to put some respect on it. So, are you finished or are you done?

Tianna - So you think you're Birdman now? Listen, I've got to go; but change Ashley's mind. You know you're the only one she listens to…kk babes love you. I'll talk to you later. (Hangs up call)

Scene 6: Ashley and Laylah argue, and Laylah confesses her feelings for Ashley

Ashley - (Walks back upstairs to use the bathroom)

Laylah - (Hears the bathroom door open, gets up and walks to the bathroom and leans in the doorway)

Ashley - (Runs bath water)

Laylah - Soo…you're just gonna take a bath without me?

Ashley - I'm not obligated to tell you my every move Lay. (In an annoyed tone)

Laylah - Yes! You are!

Ashley - (Raises eyebrows) Says who?

Laylah - Says me!

Ashley - (Crosses arms and shifts weight to one hip) And you are?…. Ohhh ok. I thought so. (Turns back to check the water temp again)

Laylah - You got me all the way fucked up girl! You better act like you know who mama is!

Ashley - Who died and made you queen?

Laylah - Bitch, the queen that died and made me queen; that's who!

Ashley - (Sucks her teeth) Whatever Lay, you are not the boss around here.

Laylah - Ummm excuse me, I am the boss. As a matter of fact, I'm the only boss, and I'm your boss, which means that you must tell me your every single move! Periodt.

Ashley - (In a sarcastic tone) Uuuhhh...I think the fuck not "Your Highness". (Rolls her eyes)

Laylah - Keep rolling your eyes...

Ashley - And if I do?

Laylah - I'ma whoop you.

Ashley - Ohhhh! I'm so scared you're gonna beat me. (Starts laughing) Girl please. You're not gonna touch me.

Laylah - Ohhh really huh? Bitch hold that thought. I'll be right back (Goes in her room and gets a belt)

Ashley - (Starts taking off her clothes getting ready to get in the tub)

Laylah - (Comes back to the bathroom and hits Ashley on her ass)

Ashley - Owwwwwww!!! (Grabs her ass cheek) Bitch that shit hurt!

Laylah - Now who's not gonna do what? (Puts hand to ear and turns it toward Ashley as if she's trying to hear her better)

Ashley - (Evilly looks at Laylah)

Laylah - Bitch I wish you would. I'll fuck your little ass up with this belt. You need your ass beat for all that damn mouth you got.

Ashley - (Rolls eyes) You think because you're a few months older than me that….(Voice trails off)

Laylah - (Interrupts Ashley cutting her off) Yup, yes I do. I'm the mother fuckin boss! Like I said! Ssoo you're gonna do what I mother fucking say, and you're going to tell me your every mother fucking move; because that's how it is and that's what I said you're going to do.

Ashley - (Being very sarcastic) Yes Drill Sargent! Whatever you say. (Starts laughing)

Laylah - (Drops the belt on the floor) No really babes; come to Tasha's Party with me.

Ashley - (Gets in the tub and sits down)

Laylah - Ashley!

Ashley - What Lay!?

Laylah - (In a demanding tone) You're coming to her party with me and I don't care what you say!

Ashley - I don't know why you want me to go so damn bad!

Laylah - Because you're my girl, and girls don't let their girls go to events alone.

Ashley - Sounds like some shit Tianna would say; and now that I think about it, you have been acting weird all day; what's going on with you?

Laylah - I like you Ash………………… I want you to be my bae. My lover, and my wifey; I want you to be mine.

Ashley - (Shocked)

Laylah - Well say something!

Ashley - Lay!!!! I don't know what to say… I mean you caught me off guard. I don't…(Voice trails off)

Laylah - You don't what?

Ashley - I don't know how to feel right now.

Laylah - Earlier you said that you like girls. Well this girl just happens to feel the same way about you.

Ashley - Lay! I…. I don't know what to feel. I mean, I just got out of a relationship.

Laylah - Yeah, with a fuckboy that didn't know your worth! Ashley, we've been best friends since kindergarten. I know everything about you. I know how to treat you. I know how to handle your emotions. I know how to love you. All I want to do is take care of you and love you like a daughter. Love you like no other and protect you like a mother. You're my everything, don't you see that?

Ashley - (Sheds a tear) Lay! Why are you doing this to me?

Laylah - What am I doing babes? I didn't know it was a crime to express my feelings to someone that I love. Please don't make me regret this.

Ashley - Give me some time to think Lay. Please. I'm so confused right now.

Laylah - Sure……I'll give you some time. (Walks out of the bathroom and comes back) Ashley, just know that I would never hurt you or do anything to jeopardize our friendship, but I couldn't take it anymore. I had to tell you how I felt. You asked what was going on with me and why I'd been acting funny all day; well holding in my feelings has been eating me inside all day. I Hope this doesn't affect our friendship. (Walks out the bathroom and into her room)

Ashley - (Thinks about what Laylah just told her and smiles extremely hard)

Laylah - (Gets on Livebook and writes a new status) **"When you accept your true feelings, staying faithful to the action is more proactive than running away from how you really feel... #feelings"** (Puts down her phone and resumes the movie)

(17 minutes later)

Ashley - (Walks in the room with the towel wrapped around her) So, you just couldn't wait for me huh? (Starts smiling)

Laylah - (Looks at Ashley and smiles) Come here girl.

Ashley - (Walks to the bed and sits down)

Laylah - So did you think about what I said?

Ashley - Yes and you're right. Girls don't let their girls go to events alone.

Laylah - So that means you're coming with me to Tasha's party?!

Ashley - Ummmm I'm still thinking about it.

Laylah - Bitch!

Ashley - Alright, alright I'll go; but I'm only going because you asked me to go. NOT because she wants me there. But I swear Lay, if she even looks at me the wrong way, it's gonna be people celebrating her death and not her life. It will quickly turn into a "happy death day Tasha."

<u>Laylah</u> - Girl Shut up!

<u>Ashley</u> - You think I'm playing? She better stay far, far away from me when we get there because, if she comes at me sideways, she's gonna catch these hands.

<u>Laylah</u> - (Laughing) Whatever girl, you always wanna fight somebody.

<u>Ashley</u> - You're damn right! As long as I got strength in my body, any bitch on this planet can catch these hands!

<u>Laylah</u> - You're crazy girl. You betta be nice before I whoop you...again. You know you're not going to do anything anyway. I won't let you, and besides, (Pulls Ashley close to her) if anybody touches you, you know I don't play that shit.

<u>Ashley</u> - You stay being overprotective over me Lay. (Blushing)

<u>Laylah</u> - Is that a problem?

<u>Ashley</u> - No, I'm just saying.

<u>Laylah</u> - You're just saying what? You better be glad I'm overprotective of your ugly ass.

<u>Ashley</u> - Girl please. Sooooo, if I'm so ugly then why do you want me?

<u>Laylah</u> - Because ugly girls turn me on.

<u>Ashley</u> - (Burst out laughing)

<u>Laylah</u> - (Starts laughing) Seriously though, it's getting late. I think we should go to bed. It's turn up day tomorrow!

<u>Ashley</u> - You're right. (Yawns) I'm getting tired anyway.

<u>Laylah</u> - Yeah, and it's way past your bedtime.

<u>Ashley</u> - (In a sarcastic tone) Yes mother. May I lay down now almighty one? (Starts smiling and lays down)

<u>Laylah</u> - You must want me to really whoop you huh girl? Keep playing with me; keep testing my kindness bitch. (Faces Ashley and lays down beside her) I love you babes.

<u>Ashley</u> - (Smiles) Love you too babes, Goodnight.

<u>Laylah</u> - Goodnight (Closes eyes)

<u>Ashley</u> - Lay?

<u>Laylah</u> - Yes Ashley?

<u>Ashley</u> - Give me time to think about what you said earlier. Ok?

<u>Laylah</u> - K babes.

<u>Scene 7: Tasha calls Tianna and aggravates her</u>

<u>Tasha</u> - (Calls Tianna)

<u>Tianna</u> - (Opens one eye and watches the phone ring) Ughhhhh what does this girl want? (Sighs)

<u>Tasha</u> - (Calls Tianna again)

Tianna - (Takes a deep breath) If this girl don't leave me alone! God! Please, just make her stop calling!

Tasha - (Calls Tianna again)

Tianna - (Wakes up and picks up the phone) Girl what do you want?!

Tasha - I can't sleep ughhhhhhhh...

Tianna - Ughhhhh (Sarcastically) I can't sleep either. (Rolls eyes)

Tasha - I hate it here!

Tianna - So why don't you leave?

Tasha - It's not that easy, and it's too damn hot. I'm wired up on chocolate and I keep fantasizing about my future. I want to accomplish two goals before I go to sleep, and I'm thinking about my birthday party that's officially 3 weeks from now. Can't you tell I have a lot on my mind?

Tianna - Girl if you don't quit. Do you know what time it is? And why is it not that easy to leave? People get up and leave all the time.

Tasha - It's not that easy because I have a life here and people I care about. I don't want to just leave like that...but then again, I do want to leave....but then again, I don't know. Uuuhgghhh! Tianna help meeee!

Tianna - Bitch you should just leave! Nobody likes you and nobody actually wants you here. What life do you have and what valid reason do you have to stay here?

Tasha - Apparently, I don't have a life at all if I'm talking to you at almost 3 in the morning. Talking bout it's difficult to move because I have a life here. (Starts laughing and shaking her head) I think I'm too hot. I'm about to turn the fan on.

Tianna - Girl bye! You irk my soul so bad; waking me up out of my sleep for this dumb convo. This could've waited until the morning. (Hangs up and goes back to sleep)

Scene 8: Ashely and Laylah get ready to go to the mall (7:00 AM)

Laylah - (Dances in the mirror holding a brush)

Ashley - (Wakes up slowly and yawns) Bitch, who are you looking cute for?

Laylah - The Father, The Son, and The Holy Ghost.

Ashley - (Yawns again) Girl bye!

Laylah - Girl, you better wake up. The mall opens at 10 and you know you take forever to get dressed.

Ashley - (Sit's up and stretches) That's because I have to actually look like something.

Laylah - So you mean to tell me that you look like nothing before you look like something?

Ashley - Uh no. (Rolls eyes) Hater. I always look like something. I'm a snack in everyone's eyes, and every bitch wishes they could either be me or be like me; but they can't because I'm just that bitch and ain't no bitch more fly than I. Periodt.

Laylah - Girl, I know all too well. I have people coming at me all the time, thinking they can do what I do. BUT, we know better and you know better, because you know me. I don't know a bitch that looks this good. I look so good that I be taking bitches from their bitches, and the bitches that be with their niggas be breaking their necks when they see me sliding through.

Ashley - Yassss bitch! Yyaassss! Looking like a whole snack!

Laylah - Okuuurrrrrrrrrrt!

Ashley - You're so ratchet!

Laylah - The word is classy. Don't kill my vibe bitch, I just got a little bit of Cardi B in me; that's it.

Ashley - (Gets up from the bed and stands next to Ashley)

Laylah - Ewwww girl, you stink! Can you say bath time?!

Ashley - Can you say mind yours? And I don't stink. I just released a silent fart.

Laylah - (Looks disgusted) Ewww bitch, take you, and your titties to the shower; stankin booty ass lil' girl.

Ashley - (Smiling) Are you coming with me?

Laylah - Next time babes; I just got out.

Ashley - So you took one without me!?

Laylah - Yup, you took a bath without me last night Ms. Attitude, did you forget?

Ashley - I needed time to myself Lay, I told you that.

Laylah - (Shrugs) So go take a shower by yourself.

Ashley - (Gives Lay an evil look and walks out of the bedroom into the bathroom)

Laylah - (Brushes her hair and stops to think about asking Ashley to move in)

Ashley - (Gets undress and takes a shower)

Laylah - (Walks out of the room and walks downstairs to the kitchen, takes food out of the fridge to start cooking breakfast)

<u>Ashley</u> - (Gets out of the shower to dry off and then loudly screams)

<u>Laylah</u> - (Stops what she's doing and runs upstairs to the bathroom) Babes! What's up?! What's wrong?! Are you ok?

<u>Ashley</u> - Oh my god Lay! Kill it, kill it, KILL IITT! (Panicking)

<u>Laylah</u> - Kill what Ashley? Calm down!

<u>Ashley</u> - (Points at the spider on the wall and screams louder)

<u>Laylah</u> - (Starts laughing while taking off her slipper to kill the spider on the wall) Oh my god Ashley. You're so tough, but you're scared of a little spider?

<u>Ashley</u> - It wasn't little!

<u>Laylah</u> - Girl. The next time you scream like that, it better not be for no damn spider! (Starts laughing and walks out of the bathroom)

<u>Ashley</u> - (Dries off and speaks under her breath) The next time I scream like that, it's going to be from you eating this pussy.

<u>Laylah</u> - (Heads back downstairs to the kitchen and starts cooking)

<u>Ashley</u> - (Walks in the room and gets dressed, sits on the bed while thinking about how she's going to wear her hair)

<u>Laylah</u> - (Finishes cooking breakfast and puts Ashley's plate in the microwave and screams upstairs) Ashleyyyyyyyyyyyyyy, hurryyyyyyyyyyyy upppppppppppppppp!

<u>Ashley</u> - (Screams back downstairs) I'm cominnnngggggggggggggggggggggggg!

Laylah - (Screams back upstairs) You need to be coming your ass down these stairs!

Ashley - (Walks downstairs into the kitchen) Mmmmm. (Closes her eyes and deeply inhales) What smells so good?

Laylah - My breakfast; (Smiles) and you can't have any.

Ashley - So, you didn't make me a plate? I don't see my plate. (Looking around the kitchen)

Laylah - You don't get a plate.

Ashley - You know what Lay? You know what?...(Voice trails off) Never mind, with your greedy, eat up all the food ass! (Standing with her arms crossed and pouting)

Laylah - What are you so uptight for? How was your shower Spider Girl? (Starts laughing)

Ashley - Shut up! You're not funny Lay. I'mmmmm hhhhungryyyyyy!!

Laylah - Well cook you some food then Ms. "Oh So Hungry"!

Ashley - Come on Lay, I just got out of the shower and I don't feel like cooking. Plus! You said I "can't" cook. Remember?!

Laylah - Well. It looks like you're just going to be hungry then Ms. "Scared of Spiders."

Ashley - Layyyyy!

Laylah - Your food is in the microwave agi!

Ashley - See! You do love me!

Laylah - Nope. I just tolerate you because I'm afraid of being alone.

Ashley - Yeah, yeah. (Gets the plate out the microwave and sits across from Laylah) Ssoooo, what time are we going to the mall?

Laylah - (Finishes eating) Uuuhhh...have you looked in the mirror lately?

Ashley - What's wrong?

Laylah - We're not going the mall with you looking like nobody takes care of you.

Ashley - I'm wearing a scarf, calm down.

Laylah - Uuhhh no you're not! I'm not letting you walk out of this house looking like who did what and why!

Ashley - But Lay?

Laylah - But Lay nothing, when you're done, meet me upstairs Ms. "I Can't Believe It's Not A Spider." (Heads upstairs)

Ashley - (Rolls eyes and finishes eating)

Scene 9: Laylah and Ashley discuss Amanda and Tianna

Laylah - (Voice calls Amanda)

Amanda - (Picks up) Yyyaassssss bitch! I was just thinking about you mama.

Laylah - Y'all still going to the mall?

Amanda - Yea, I'm just waiting for Tianna to call me back.

Laylah - Ohhhhhh, you'e bringing Tianna with you?

Amanda - Yeah, you know she's my bitch.

Laylah - Yeah, yeah, she's cool, I guess. She was over here last night asking for money.

Amanda - I know, she told me that you gave her $100. I was going to ask why, but girl you know I'm not finna get in the middle of that.

Laylah - I swear, (voice trails off) why is she telling my business? Did she also tell you that she begged me to give her that money?!

Amanda - Girl you know Tianna has issues.

Laylah - Apparently big ones; enough of that though. What time are you trying to meet at the mall? I'm trying to leave around 10. I'm waiting for Ashely to come upstairs so I can do her hair. You know she thinks she's the flyest thing moving.

<u>Ashley</u> - (Walks in the room)

<u>Laylah</u> - Girl speaking of the devil. Ashley just walked in. I'ma see you at the mall. (Hangs up)

<u>Ashley</u> - Who was that? (Sits on the bed)

<u>Laylah</u> - Girl, that was nobody but Amanda.

<u>Ashley</u> - I don't like Amanda.

<u>Laylah</u> - Girl, who do you like? I swear you don't like anybody.

<u>Ashley</u> - I don't! Everybody irks my lifeline!

<u>Laylah</u> - Well Amanda and Tianna are going to meet us at the mall.

<u>Ashley</u> - Uh no, they better not be at the mall Lay; or I'm telling you now, I'm running up on Amanda and that's word to my DNA. I can't stand that bitch! I hate her even more than I hate Tasha!

<u>Laylah</u> - (Looks at Ashley) Girl something is clearly wrong with you.

<u>Ashley</u> - Yup, I hate bitches! That's what's wrong with me. Ouhhhhhh, (Gets mad) now I wanna fight!

<u>Laylah</u> - You better chill out.

<u>Ashley</u> - No Lay, these bitches irk me to the point that my soul wants to hop out of my body just to beat their asses.

<u>Laylah</u> - (Laughs) Girl, come sit between my legs so I can take care of that hair of yours.

<u>Ashley</u> - Lay I'm serious. If I see Amanda, it's on sight; so you better warn the bitch. (Sits between Laylah's legs)

Laylah - (Starts doing Ashley's hair) Girl! Do you know that Tianna is telling people I gave her money?

Ashley - No really? (Sarcastically) I told you, she ain't nothing but a leech! I'm starting not to like her either.

Laylah - You're really bugged Ash.

Ashley - No, all she does is take advantage of you, and you don't see it, and that irks me.

Laylah - Ashley, I think you're starting to develop trust issues.

Ashley - Yup, trust issues with those bitches that I don't like. Tianna is a leeching snake. Tasha is a man stealer who can't fight, and Amanda is just phony as shit, miserable, and has no life. My energy shifts to negative when I'm around any of them. I can tell they're all jealous of me.

Laylah - And, you know this how?

Ashley - Look at how they act around me; you can't tell? I think you need glasses because obviously, you're not paying attention to the clear signs they're showing. They only fuck with me because of what you do for them. They're fake as hell, and their lives are operating on borrowed time. They so desperately wish they could be you, so they come around just because, and then they talk shit about you behind your back. Their lives are just sad as shit, and I will fuck all of those bitches up. Point blank, periodt.

Laylah - Girl, you need Jesus!

Ashley - The hell I do! Jesus told me to throw these hands when I see them, so that's what I'm going to do. Starting with Amanda's ass. That's on her mizzy borrowed life; I'm fucking her up; and if Tianna's leeching ass wants some, then she can get it too! I got time today.

Laylah - (Finishes with Ashley's hair) Girl you are not gonna do anything. Your ass stay trying to fight.

Ashley - And, so what? I don't like none of them fake bitches. Their lives are so corny, and they're all broke with nothing going on. (Gets up and looks in the mirror) Oh my god Lay! Girl, you did it again. (Starts striking poses) Bitches hate knowing they can't look this good.

Laylah - Are you ready to go to the mall now Ms. Tough Girl?

Ashley - Lay, I swear to whatever the highest power is that's fucking up those mizzy bitches lives! If I see them at the mall it's a wrap! I'm telling you. I'm taking no prisoners and raising all hell. Satan is gonna be so mad that I'm doing his job for him.

Laylah - (Starts laughing and gets up) Girl; you're a trip, come on, let's go.

Ashley - I'm fly as shit, and these bitches are just hating ass birds. I'ma be breaking necks today. Let a bitch get it twisted and I'ma smack the shit out of them.

Laylah - Girl. Come on with your angry, fly, cute ass. (Walks downstairs, and out the door to get in the car)

Ashley - (Looks in the mirror again and adjusts her clothes, walks downstairs out the door and gets in the car)

Scene 10: Ashley and Laylah head to the mall

Laylah - Don't get to the mall acting all stupid Ashley.

Ashley - Can't make any promises Lay.

Laylah - We're finally here, please just act right for once Ash.

Ashley - I can't wait for a bitch to look at me sideways; they got the game fucked up.

Laylah - Calm down Ms. "I Can't Wait To Beat A Bitch Up."

Ashley - Look over there (Pointing to Amanda and Tianna walking into the mall) at those two mizzy ass bitches.

Laylah - Ashley!!!!!!!! Be nice!!

Ashley - (Takes deep breath) Ok…but only for ten minutes.

Laylah - Ashely!!! (Starts laughing)

Ashley - Ok, ok, alright I'll behave….maybe.

Laylah - Bitch, you better! With your crazy ass! (Gets out the car and starts walking towards the mall entrance)

Ashley - (Thinks of how she's gonna handle the situation when she sees Amanda and Tianna up close and gets out the car) Lay…. You just gon leave me like that?

Laylah - (Looks back) Bitch don't you have two legs? You can catch up.

Ashley - (Smirks and struts toward the mall entrance like a model on the runway)

Laylah - Ok. Ashley the model, I see you.

Ashley - Tah, time to make a scene in here.

Laylah - Ashley!

Ashley - Ok I'll be nice……. for now!

Laylah - (Takes out her phone and calls Tianna)

Tianna - (Picks up) Hello.

Laylah - Bitch, where are you at?

Tianna - We're at the food court about to get some chicken wings.

Laylah - Ohhhh ok, we're coming to y'all now.

Tianna - We? Who is we?

Laylah - Me, and my bae.

Tianna - Oh Nah, you boo loving today? Aaaww, how cute!

Laylah - Girl bye, you wish you had a bae like mine.

Tianna - Nobody wants a self-centered, shit talking, clingy, immature ass bitch like Ashley. Sorry boo boo, you are sadly mistaking.

Laylah - You forgot gorgeous as fuck, you ugly creature.

Ashley - (Stands there impatiently)

Tianna - Girl bye. (Hangs up the phone)

Ashley - Sooooooo. Where are they?

Laylah - Ughhhh at times I hate Tianna.

Ashley - What did she do now?

Laylah - Nothing, (sighs deeply) they're at the food court eating chicken wings.

Ashley - Let's go! (Quickly walks inside of the mall)

Laylah - Bitch who do you think you're rushing!?

Ashley - Nobody. I'm just saying come on.

Scene 11: Ashley and Laylah approach Amanda and Tianna

(Ashley and Laylah walk up to the table where Amanda and Tianna are eating)

Laylah - Ssooo y'all greedy bitches couldn't order us any food?

Ashley - (Sits down and takes a chicken off of Tianna's tray and starts eating it)

Tianna - Bitch! Excuse you!

Ashley - You're excused bitch!

Laylah - Come on don't start. Ashley I'ma get us some chicken since these hoes don't want to share. (Leaves and go to the food court and stands in line for chicken)

Ashley - (Eating the chicken) Girl how much did you pay for this? (Sarcastically)

Amanda - So you're not going to say anything Ashley?

Ashley - (Rolls eyes)

Amanda - Fuck you too bitch!

Ashley - Amanda, I'm asking you nicely; do not say anything to me; please and thank you!

Amanda - You can leave with your stank attitude having ass. Nobody invited you here anyway.

Ashley - Ahhhh I Invited myself here; and you're gonna do what? Oh ok. I thought so.

Amanda - Tianna, get your girl.

Ashley - Or what? What are you gonna do besides sit your ass there and eat that chicken? I know good and damn well that you're not gonna touch me.

Amanda - Little girl, I don't know who you think you're talking to.

Ashley - (Gets up erratically) Bitch I'm talking to you! You're mad as fuck right now; ahhhhh haaaa!! You ain't gonna do shit to me!

Amanda - Tianna on her life you better get this little girl away from me!

Ashley - Your ol' G.E.D having ass shouldn't be talking to bitches with actual high school Diplomas!

Tianna - Ashley, you need to chill.

Ashley - I need to chill? No baby girl; YOU need to chill! You ain't got no money, you broke as shit, you have no life, and you can't keep a nigga. You're a thot and a whole slut! Always talking about somebody. I should beat your ass too! You fake ass, using ass bitch.

Amanda - (Calmly) Ashley. I think you should go.

Ashley - Bitch you not gone make me, and I'm not going; thank you very much!

Tianna - You're sooo immature!

Ashley - Play with me if you want to bitch, and these immature paws are gonna beat you into a hospital bed.

Tianna - (Looks at Ashley)

Amanda - Tianna, don't waste your time on this little girl.

Ashley - Any bitch that has an opinion can suck my dick! (Knocks the trays off the table)

Tianna - (Gets up) Ashley, what's your problem?

Laylah - (Runs toward the table) Ashley chill out!

Ashley - No, fuck these bitches!

Tianna - Who are you calling a bitch?

Ashley - I'm talking to you!

Tianna - Lay, get your girl before I hurt her.

Ashley - You're not gonna do shit to me. I double dare you to try hoe! You're mad cause I get money. You're salty as fuck that I handle my own; meanwhile, you stay with your hand out with your begging, broke ass; and that's the truth!

Amanda - (Gets up) Little girl! I'm warning you!

Ashley -This life shit is not a game! Don't play with me cause I ain't come here to play with none of y'all corny bitches. So wassup?! Either you're going to do something, or you're going to get the fuck out of my face!

Amanda - (Spits at Ashley)

Ashley - (Dodges the spit) Bitch! (Jumps over the table and starts punching Amanda in her face continuously) Bitch, you have lost your god damn mind! The audacity!! (Starts bashing her head against the floor continuously)

Laylah - Babes chill!!! (Grabs Ashley off of Amanda)

Ashley - No, fuck that bitch. Ol' ugly G.E.D having ass hoe!

Tianna - (Checks on Amanda) Lay girl, get that psycho out of here!

Ashley - I'll beat your scary fake ass too!

Laylah - Ashley!!!! (Tosses Ashley back) I told you not to start anything!

Ashley - I was trying to be nice Lay, but those fake ass bitches irk me so bad. Lay, you don't even understand! I told that bitch not to say anything to me! I warned her! Warning comes before destruction, and now that bitch will always remember to take heed to that warning.

Tianna - (Looks at Ashley with a scared look on her face)

Ashley - Fuck you gonna do huh?! You little scary ass leech!

Laylah - Let's go Ash.(Grabs Ashley's arm, and starts pulling her away from the scene) You told me you were gonna behave babes.

Ashley - Those are your fake ass friends Lay! Get off of me! (Tries to pull away)

Laylah - No, I'm taking you back home!

Ashley - Get off me Lay! Let go!

Laylah - I said let's go! (Pulls Ashley harder) I'm not letting go until your mean ass calms down!

Ashley - (Stops resisting and relaxes)

Laylah - (Walks out of the mall and let's go of Ashley) Girl I can't believe you! Why in the world would you embarrass me like that? Do you know how crazy you look? You're lucky nobody called the cops on your dumb angry ass!

Ashley - (Walks to the car angry) Fuck that bum ass hoe and her ugly begging ass friend. I hate both of them bitches! They can both suck my pussy on a bloody day! (gets in the car and slams the door)

Laylah - (Gets in the car and takes a deep breath)

(Drives home in silence)

Scene 12: Layla and Ashley get home and talk more about what happened at the mall

Ashley - (Gets out the car and slams the door)

Laylah - (Gets out the car) Ashley you need to calm down. It's over! Leave what happened at the mall - at the mall! (opens her house door and walks inside)

Ashley - (Walks in behind her) You have no idea how mad I am. But I'm pissed that you stopped me Lay!

Laylah - Girl you better be lucky I stopped you. You were about to murder ol' girl!

Ashley - Good! That bitch deserves to die!

Laylah - Ashley!!!!

Ashley - No, she really does! She was telling fake ass Tianna to tell me that I better get out of her face. Ouuhhhhhhh! I can't wait until Kayla comes back from vacation. She's gonna laugh her ass off when I tell her what happened.

Laylah - Girl I told you to chill, and Kayla is not going to know what happened; cause you're not going to tell her!

Ashley -Yeah ok.

Laylah - You heard what I said!

Ashley - (Smirks) You think you run me?

Laylah - Duh, bitch I do!

Ashley - You are not my mother Lay! (Rolls eyes)

Laylah - (Raises voice) Bitch, who do you think you're talking to?!

Ashley - Nobody!

Laylah - Bitch that's what I thought. I'm not Amanda! Don't get shit twisted; I'll beat your little ass!

Ashley - (Smirks) You promise?

Laylah - Keep taking me for a joke girl.

Ashley - (Smiles) Lay, when is Kayla and Jasmine coming back from their vacation?

Laylah - I don't know. Remind me to call Jasmine later. I haven't spoken to her since she left. Don't think you're off the hook though; you have yet to feel my wrath. Making me look wild and crazy at the mall. What the fuck were you thinking?...Nah, don't answer that. I know you weren't' thinking. You just wanted to do what Ashley wanted to do!

Ashley - Lay!!!!

Laylah - Don't Lay me... I'm mad at you! (Heads in the kitchen)

Ashley - Layyyyyyyyyyyyyyy! (Follows her into the kitchen) Please don't be mad at me!

Laylah - (Ignores Ashley)

Ashley - Layyyyy!!

Laylah - (Ignores Ashley)

Ashley - (Gets irritated and walks out of the kitchen and up the stairs)

Laylah - (Starts making lunch for her and Ashley)

Ashley - (Walks into the bedroom and starts scrolling on Livebook and sees Tianna's post)

Tianna's post:
"Bitches have nothing better to do than to start shit because they have nothing better to do with their miserable lives. On my way to the hospital for my bitch Amanda."

Ashley - (Starts laughing) I hope that bitch dies with her ugly ass!

Laylah - (Walks into the bedroom with two plates) Get off Livebook and eat.

Ashley - (Closes Livebook and grabs the plate)

Laylah - (Sits on the bed) Give me your phone, you're not allowed to be on it for the rest of today; I'm putting you on punishment.

Ashley - Lay you're taking this too far.

Laylah - Am I really? It's either you give me your phone or I don't talk to you. I'll even allow you to choose boo.

Ashley - Ughhhhh (Gives Lay her phone) here, you happy?

Laylah - Very, I still can't believe what you did at the mall. (Shakes her head)

Ashley - So what! I told you before we left that I was going to put that bitch in her place and I did just that; now she's on her way to the hospital. I hope she dies there.

Laylah - You know you're evil right?

Ashley - Yup, the devil came and took my soul last night when I was taking a bath. He was like "daughter, come join me, on the dark side and Lay will always be by your side like Nationwide." (Starts laughing)

Laylah - (Starts laughing) Girl I can't with you, so how do you know she's on her way to the hospital?

Ashley - Live book!

Laylah - No!

Ashley - Yes bitch! Tianna's bum ass posted that she was going to the hospital for Amanda's stupid ass. You know she subbed me right? Talkin' bout I don't have anything better to do with my life than to cause trouble. Bitch! You don't even have a life, and you're always begging! Fuck outta here talking shit with your ugly ass.

Laylah - No she didn't, you didn't reply did you?

Ashley - Lay, girl I swear it was taking every bone in my soul less body not to say anything back. Lord knows I wanted to so bad though!

Laylah - Well, I'm glad you didn't. We don't need your satanic ass stirring up anymore shit.

Ashley - Hope that bitch dies, and Tianna gets hit by a truck!

Laylah - (Burst out laughing) God, please forgive her for she knows not what she does. Girl, what did they ever do to you?

Ashley - Ummmm let me see they were born, they are alive, and they talk shit about people they know they can't beat!

Laylah - Oh Lord! Jesus, please take the wheel!

Ashley - Yup! Jesus take the wheel and let it be the wheel of a truck so I can run Tianna's begging ass over, so she can then beg you for the life she never had!

Laylah - Listen, (Finishes her food trying not to laugh) you need help like for real girl. We're going to get you evaluated. It's going to be alright. I promise.

Ashley - Bitch you think it's funny?

Laylah - No. I think you're possessed! You do hear what you're saying right?

Ashley - No. I'm talking just to be talking. The only thing I wanna hear is Tianna's bones cracking when she gets hit by that truck. Fuck that bitch! I can't stand her!

Laylah - Well, I'm going downstairs to find a pastor girl; cause all of this negative energy you're holding on to is not safe. I feel like the demons are taking over my baby.

Ashley - (Starts speaking in a demonic Voice) Join us! (starts laughing)

Laylah - Ohhh hell no bitch! You're definitely tripping! Now give me your plate.

Ashley - (Hands lay the plate) You're so scary Lay. You need to learn how to take a joke.

Laylah - Nope you're crazy...with your psycho ass. (Gets up and starts heading downstairs)

Ashley - Layyyyyyyyy, give me back my ppphhoonnneee.

Laylah - Noooooo! With your crazy ass.

<u>Ashley</u> - Layyyyyyyyyyyyyyyyyyyyyyyyyyyyyyyyyyyyyyyyyyyyy!

<u>Laylah</u> - Noooooooooooooooooooooooooooooooooo!

<u>Ashley</u> - I can't surviveeeeeeeeeeeeeee without my phoneeeeeeeeeee!!

<u>Laylah</u> - Better start talking to the spirits then Rosemary.

<u>Ashley</u> - Layyyyyyyyyyyyyyy!

<u>Laylah</u> - (Ignores Ashley and walks downstairs into the kitchen)

<u>Ashley</u> - (Turns on the T.V and watches Movieflix)

<u>Laylah</u> - (Puts the plates in the sink, takes out her phone, and starts to call jasmine)

<u>Jasmine's voicemail</u> - "Hello, you've reached Jasmine. I can't come to my phone right now leave your name, and number, and I'll get back to you. Peace and blessings"

<u>Laylah</u> - Bitchhhhhhhhhhh callllll meeeeee back whenever you get this. It's very important; like urgently important! Bye!

Scene 13: Ashely kisses Laylah and tells her she wants to take it to another level

<u>Ashley</u> - (Walks into the kitchen pouting) Layyyyyyyyyyyyyy give me back my phone.

<u>Laylah</u> - Noooooooooooo psycho.

<u>Ashley</u> - Please don't make me beg you because I will!

<u>Laylah</u> - You're such a big baby.

<u>Ashley</u> - (Walks up to Laylah) I'm your big baby though.

<u>Laylah</u> - Unfortunately, you're lucky I love your……….(Voice trails off)

<u>Ashley</u> - (Kisses Laylah on the lips, and looks into her eyes)

<u>Laylah</u> - Girl what are you do………

<u>Ashley</u> - (Kisses Laylah again on the lips more passionately shutting her up)

<u>Laylah</u> - (Smiles)

<u>Ashley</u> - I want you!

<u>Laylah</u> - You want me?

<u>Ashley</u> - I want you……to give me back my phone…. Lay come on; you're killing me!

<u>Laylah</u> - Bitch, you play too much! Get out of my face.

<u>Ashley</u> - Make me!

<u>Laylah</u> - Girl, don't play with me.

<u>Ashley</u> - Like I said. Make me!

<u>Laylah</u> - I can't with you.

<u>Ashley</u> - Layyyyyyyyyy mami.

Laylah - Oh; now I'm Mami huh?

Ashley - Yes. (Kisses her again on the lips and sucks on her bottom lip)

Laylah - (Grabs Ashley by her ponytail) Since when? (kisses Ashley deeply and passionately)

Ashley - (Bites her lip) Since now.

Laylah - Oh really?

Ashley - Yes really. I've been thinking about what you said last night.

Laylah - Really?

Ashley - Yes! I want you as much as you want me.

Laylah - Nope too late. You should've wanted me last night when I wanted you. I've since then changed my mind.

Ashley - Layyyyyyyyyyyy!

Laylah - (Smiles) I'm just playing baby cakes.

Ashley - I love you too.

Laylah - (Smiles and pushes Ashley away) Nice try; but you still aren't getting your phone back.

Ashley - Ughhhhh, I hate youuuuuuu!

Laylah - Oh really? (Grabs Ashley's ass and pulls her close) You hate me?

Ashley - No.

Laylah - No what?

Ashley - No mami.

Laylah - Good girl, now get out of my face; you're still on punishment.

Ashley - Layyyyy, but I'm being a good girl.

Laylah - Really?

Ashley - Yes. I'm being a great girl! See? (Smiles) If I were an angel, there would be a halo shining above me right now.

Laylah - But, you're not. I can actually see your devil horns, Ms. Spawn of Satan.

Ashley - Lay, no for reals.

Laylah - What?

Ashley - I really thought about it. You know? What you were saying last night...

Laylah - Mmmmhhhhhhmmmmmm...aannnddd?

Ashley - You make a lot of sense.

Laylah - Oh do I now?

Ashley - Yes. You do.

Laylah - Andddddd?...

Ashley - And, I think I need the type of love that you're offering to give me.

Laylah - (Kisses Ashley)

Ashley - So are we together?

Laylah - Are you asking me to be yours?

Ashley - Are you saying yes?

Laylah - Are you asking?

Ashley - Yes.

Laylah - Yes what? (Smiles)

Ashley - Yes, I want to be yours, and I'm asking you to be mine.

Laylah - (Kisses Ashley)

Ashley - (Kisses Lay back)

Laylah - You still aren't getting your phone back.

Ashley - Layyyy! Come on!

Laylah - Nopeeee

Ashley - Ugh! Bye! (Walks out the kitchen pouting)

Laylah - You madddddd ugly! (Laughing)

Ashley - Hater.

Laylah - That's why you aren't getting your phone back. Keep playing and I'll make it two days.

Ashley - Why play with the phone when I have you to play with? (Strikes a pose and walks upstairs)

Laylah - Girl! You know your ass is sexy!

Ashley - And, you know it. Okurttttttttttt!

Laylah - (Screams upstairs) loveeeeee youuuuuuuuu!

Ashley - (Screams downstairs) hateeeeee youuuuuu!

Scene 14: Kayla calls Laylah and tells her that Amanda's in a coma and Tianna is plotting to get rid of Ashley

Laylah - (Starts washing the dishes and hears her phone ringing, dries her hands off and answers) Hello.

Kayla - Girl, have you been on Livebook?

Laylah - Nope. I just got back home. Why? What's going on?

Kayla - What did that angry bird Ashley do now, because Tianna's going crazy; talking about how she's gonna get revenge, and that Amanda's in a coma, and how it's crazy that bitches will let their friends fight over nothing…Hold up girl, Jasmine is on the other line I'ma click her in.

Jasmine - Bitch, what did Ashley do?

Laylah - You were supposed to call me back hoe!

Kayla - Oh my god! (Getting worried) What happened at the mall Lay?

Laylah - (Sighs deeply)

Jasmine - Yeah Lay, what happened? Why is Amanda in a coma?

Laylah - Long story short...

Kayla - Let me guess, (Kayla interrupts) the angry bird got mad and went black on Amanda.

Jasmine - Lay, girl tell me that's not what happened?

Kayla - Lay, you know you're supposed to keep her in check cause you know she's a major hot head!

Laylah - Y'all act like it's my fault Amanda got beat into a coma!

Kayla - If not yours, then whose fault is it Lay? Where were you?

Laylah - It's her fault she got her ass beat. I was minding my business; getting chicken. I told Ashley not to do anything.

Jasmine - Girl, now you know Ashley has a mind of her own and doesn't listen to reason.

Kayla - Yeah girl, you know Ashley has serious issues.

Laylah - Y'all better leave my bae alone.

Jasmine - (Gasp) Whoa! So you're fucking Ashley now?

Kayla - Girl, they were an item before they were an item. Where have you been?

Jasmine - Apparently unaware of what's going on because I be minding my own; Shakkaayyllaa!

Kayla - I know you didn't just say my government like that Little Jazzy! You're just mad because I went to the pool without you earlier.

Laylah - Y'all can kiss and make up on your own time. Sssooooo, what's going on? I know y'all got tea.

Kayla - Shut up Ms. I'm Boo'ed Up Now, but yeah, Tianna is plotting on Ashley for putting Amanda's hating, fake ass in a coma. I don't know what she's talking about doing, but she's lucky I'm not there.

Jasmine - Yasssss. That bitch is so lucky we aren't there. But even still, ain't nobody touching Lil Ashley without having to see me about it. Period!

Laylah - Oh trust baby, I wish Tianna would pull some shit concerning Ashley, she's gonna have to fight me first!

Kayla - That dumb bitch gonna fuck around and get jumped when we come back home. (Starts laughing) I can't stand Tianna's ugly ass.

Jasmine - Right, right. Who the fuck does her stank ass think she is? Posting that shit on Livebook like we weren't going to see it!

Laylah - Girl, I don't know but whatever is going on in her mind needs to stop and reroute. She knows she isn't about that life. Ouhhhh girl! Ya'll should have seen the look on her face after Ashley blacked out on Amanda's bitch ass. That bitch looked like she saw a ghost. She was scared as shit!

Jasmine - I bet her scary ass did see a ghost. She saw Amanda's spirit flying; I know she was terrified. She ain't want no smoke with Ashley.

Laylah - Girl, I swear I was scared for Amanda

Kayla - Girl for what?!

Laylah - Because I thought she was going to kill her. The way she was bashing her head on the floor after beating her face in; (Shutters) oh my god it was horrible to watch!

Jasmine - Speaking of the queen of angry bitches. Where is she?

Laylah - Girl, she's upstairs; mad I took her phone. I put that ass on punishment for two days, and now she's going crazy. (Laughs)

Jasmine - You know that girl can't live without her phone. (Laughs)

Kayla - I'm surprised she gave it to you. Why are you the only one who seems to be able to control her?

Laylah - Because, I'm her mother, and I got the juice like that. She knows what it is.

Jasmine - You stopped talking to her huh?

Laylah - Girl, you already know! (Bursts out laughing) I gave her little ass a choice; either give me the phone or I was done talking. Her ass was going crazy trying to get that shit back. But when do y'all plan on coming back?

Jasmine - Whenever Shakayla's light skinned ass stops being indecisive about when she wants to come back.

Kayla - Bitch! No girl, Little Miss Jazzy over here keeps saying "let's stay a few more days; we're not missing anything. But then my ass gets on Livebook, and it's like we missed a whole damn movie! WITH commercials!

Laylah - (Laughing) We miss y'all. It's so boring here. I'm around fake ppl all damn day. I need my bitches.

Jasmine - Miss Thang, ain't you in boo loving mode and all up in your feelings with "Ms. Beat A Bitch Into A Coma" over there?

Laylah - That's different, and stop talking about my bae like that before I get mad.

Kayla - Yeah Jazzy, stop talking her bae like that. Can't you tell she's all in love and shit?

(All starts laughing simultaneously)

Laylah - Yup! In love and proud of it! Hating ass bitches. (Still laughing)

Jasmine - Ewww. I think I'ma throw up!

Laylah - I smell a hater on the phone with us Kay.

Ashley - (Walks in the living room pouting) Please give me my phone. Ughhhhh I'm going crazy Lay.

Laylah - You hear this? She's asking for her phone back.

Ashley - Who are you on the phone with?

Laylah - None of your business. (Puts the phone on speaker) Say "hiiii!"

Jasmine - Hey mamas!

Kayla - Ashley! You know good and damn well you need to stop causing trouble while we aren't there to defend you!

Ashley - (Screams) My bitches…. Oh my god! Y'all need to come back home; I miss y'all! Lay's ass is over here putting me through hell!

Laylah - Un huh; like you don't deserve it.

Jasmine - We hear you're on punishment.

Kayla - Yeah bitch, no phone for you for two days ahhhhaaaaaaa!!

Ashley - Shutup, both of y'all assess!

Laylah - Be nice before I make it three days.

Ashley - Do y'all hear this?

Jasmine - Welp, sounds like you'd better be nice mamas. You know Laylah isn't playing.

Kayla - Yeah bitch, you better listen to your mother. (Laughing)

Laylah - You heard them Ashley, you'd better listen to your mother. (Smiles)

Ashley - (Smirks and rolls her eyes) Whatever, I hate all three of y'all.

Jasmine - Awwww don't hate us because YOU'RE in timeout. You're the one over there beating up bitches and leaving them helpless and shit.

Ashley - Huh? Wait, What happened now?

Kayla - Girl! You put Amanda's ass in a coma!

Ashley - (Shocked) Noooo wwaayyy!! Really?! Aaaayyyeeeee!! (Jumps in excitement)

Laylah - (Gives Ashley a mean look) That's not cute bitch.

Ashley - (Sticks tongue out) Aayyeeee! (Starts singing and dancing) I put bitches in comas; I put them in comas! I fucked her face up I bashed her head in! (Starts doing happy dance)

Laylah - Ashley!

Jasmine - Girl, you know Tianna's plotting on you; right?

Ashley - That begging ass bitch is not gonna touch me! I wish a bitch would.com. I'll become employee of fucking her face up for the month; just like I did Amanda's ass.

Laylah - (Laughs) This girl ain't got no damn sense.

Kayla - (Laughs) I don't know how you put up with her bitch.

Laylah - (Smiles) I don't know either.

Ashley - It's because she loves me.

Jasmine - Y'all can have a ball talking, but I'm about to get in this pool cause a bitch like me needs to relax ok? So, I'll holla at you later Lay, and you need to keep Ashley away from her phone for a week.

Ashley - Ohhhhh! Like Ms. Thompson did to you when we were in the 5th Grade.

Jasmine - And that smart ass mouth of yours is exactly why you're on punishment now! Aahhhhhhhhhhhh haaaaaaaaa... Bye, bitch, I'll call you later. (Hangs up)

Kayla - Yeah Lay, we'll just call you on three way again. But Ashley, I feel for you girl. I honestly would've done the same thing to Amanda though.

Laylah - Sssooo...you're just going to encourage her like that?

Ashley - Thank you girl; (Looks at Lay) at least someone understands.

Laylah - (Rolls eyes)

Kayla - Alright mamas, I'ma talk to you later.

Laylah - Bye bitch. (Hangs up)

Ashley - You're always hating.

Laylah - Nooo, you always think it's cute to act the way you act; but ain't nothing cute about it.

Ashley - You're soooo paranoid. Can you say agi much!? Ugh!

Laylah - Uuummm... can you say jail time!?

Ashley - Relax; ain't nothing going to happen to me.

Laylah - Bitch you put another girl in a coma, at the mall, a VERY public place!

Ashley - Andddddd your point is what? Did she die? No? Alright then. She will live; bitch calm down!

Hears a bang on the door

Laylah - (Goes to the door) Who is it?

A police officer responds - Q Town police, we need to question Ms. Ashley Marie, in regards to what happened at the Q Town Mall this morning.

Ashley - (Frighteningly looks at Laylah in shock)

To be continued....

<u>Dedicated to the circle of friends and the circle of possibilities that makes the circle of life more meaningfully important. Through true friendship; the circle will always remain.</u>